Monkey Time

To Kate,
me na know wa gwan but
me sign dis volume —
with bestest —
Philip Nikolayev

Feb. 6, 2008

Philip Nikolayev

Monkey Time

Winner of the 2001 Verse Prize

Verse Press
Amherst, MA

Published by Verse Press

Library of Congress Cataloging-in-Publication Data

Nikolayev, Philip.
Monkey time / Philip Nikolayev.-- 1st ed.
    p. cm.
ISBN 0-9703672-9-5 (alk. paper)
I. Title.
PS3614.I55M66 2003
811'.6--dc21

                                                    2003009883

The author of *Monkey Time* wishes to thank the editors of the following periodicals, in which some of these poems first appeared: *The Café Review, A Chide's Alphabet, The Cortland Review, CultureFront, The Dark Horse, The Formalist, Grand Street, The Indian P.E.N., Jacket, overland, The Paris Review, Quarterly West, Salt, 6x6, Slope, Stand,* and *Verse.*

Special thanks to Lyn Hejinian for choosing *Monkey Time* as the winner of the 2001 Verse Prize.

Book designed and composed by Anastasia Bogushevsky-Gareginyan.

Text and display set in 10pt Goudy Old Style and 7pt Georgia fonts.

Cover art: a detail of "Dressing Table" by Samuel Gareginyan.
Used by permission of the artist.

Printed in Canada

9 8 7 6 5 4 3 2 1

First Edition

for Katia Kapovich

CONTENTS

BOXES

Boxes are hoaxes of the imagination,
they fold out backwards
and proceed to foreclose themselves
from the other side
so as to afford a view, a purview.
Last night I stared into a box,
I was like a box within a box,
boxed in by a larger boxing.
To establish the level of nesting
-is never possible. I can box my way
out of a wet paper bag, but
bags are no boxes. I couldn't bag my way into
a dry paper box. The plastic toy-box
my daughter likes to play with
at her nine months of age shines
with a transparency
no critic has yet dared to problematize.
Clear rolls a red ball on the gray carpet.
In the box of our spring trespassing magnolias
in morganatic obsession bow to us,
they linger in our miracle lens,
white and wide void
of hope. Have you seen them?
And lines by an atrabilious bastard
(by a sky-flecked seascape)
that cause tears to flow
and cheers to follow
and wonder where the seagulls go,
and where the swallow,
and where the mast,
all packed away into boxes of memory?
I open them and close them as I please,
as if they were divine.
As the cockles of my heart click
with boxes of expectation, so
the bottleneck of proclivity
simply turns to the shoebox at the entrance,
pulls at the right shoestrings.
The flowers are still on the floor.
And then all those boxes of books,
containers of knowledge
in the basement. Why
do we keep them? Boxes breathe peace.
A blue fox in a black box is unknowable.

COMMUNICATIONS

Take a landscape, an American landscape
strewn across with seagulls jiving on the wing, take
intruding on formal precincts the only
hope of rain without windows on the west
side, sallow velocities to tower
in this life and echo of urban development,
orange blazers masterminding what I don't know.
Grids upon garbage cans upon grids,
windows east, glass obsessed, savings last,
the telephone unknowing me licks the dust, looks wiped
out. Epitaphs plug the holes of Henry Moore.
Neoned ebony elbows, tables turning, lamentable.
Businesses are business, the cave police
know the racket, take care. Compacted corridors of sense
stretch subways of refuge, deep and secretive.
Sentences of recompense, doors, flat enormities of post
suburbia. The seagulls, they jive like this,
towering, hovering, towering, hovering way out.
What's your scroblem, mister?
I no understand whuddya sayin. Bee Em W my ass.
I be livin a fifteen years this neighborhood.
The area is familiar to me. I come from not far from here.
Fortunes riding high on the American 4320 crawler crane
with a skyhorse attachment,
I have no moment to explain
voices, voices overheard of sirens,
bloody blue against a low-slit Sunday sky.
I'm crashing you shit to your face,
telling it like it is, my gentlemen and friends.
Take a pillar, a pillar of snow,
by where the holy river Hudson wags her bridges
above the great divide of dialect.
You look really Norwegian, like a Norwegian from Norway,
caught in this turnstile, this multicentric alterity
of an organism. I must misundertake the duty
to tell you which way I'm going and which I'm not,
and where I am not coming from.
Blowfish are sharks in an ocean of determination.
The thoroughfare runs on and turns to cloverleaf.
Even in our spatiotemporal catastrophe
I whisper to you through my two lips of anguish:
take a language, take an English language...

CRYSTALS CLOSED, SONNET IMMURED

Form is a sense-formative grid that sleeps within a figured object. Its impact assimilates to an extent the word crafter's work to aspects of both the jeweler's and the mason's. Rather coincidentally, *Confused and scattered, though intent to pass* over here in the right *with accurate colors your examination* hand margin I thought I *trinkets under your magnifying glass* would mention that life itself *face their ordeal in gleaming contemplation,* is foreshortened and *of many-faceted appeal. They wink* carefully foregrounded by the *into your eye, teasing your visual sense* said jeweler mason's hand, *about the wavelike ironies that link* an abstract vision working *their universe to your crystalline lens.* upon primordial matter. We *Black coffee cools forgotten. Your hair frames* are being crafted, *with its cascading and red-auburn flames* being exercised. Who is *your grandmother's near-sighted alexandrite* to say we're not up to *shifting its hues, her Jewish freckles, right* grasping, to plumbing *along with your own independent glow* - the sweep / dimension of *another smile three centuries ago.* that that distinguishes life/death? I throw enjambments in a house with sonnet windows. Sonnets may crack, but they never break. It's so unnecessary to make every facet polished. Let's leave some materials in the glint of their natural state.

INSECTS IN AMBER

What is immorality? Recent research confirms that DNA can be
extracted from insects ensnared in the resin of ancient trees. These
fossilized inclusions are preserved magnificently, quite unscratched,
A friend of the Forms, yet I'm hurt by what their genes attached
Plato so influentially taught into the bargain. Today, you can buy
concerning poetry. His words again a wee forty million year old
fill me with such illuminating pain ant with a partial cockroach
that clear of sleep, on humming wings I wander in glows of gold,
into a moon-infested park to ponder which proves even part roach
the logos, anxious to concede its truth. is true art beyond reproach
It's time to shed the innocence of youth (but it takes a long time to
about this. Poets are cicadas. Reader, gel.) Today it's easy to find
see how I've trilled a figure for you in meter, early to mid Geno-
purveying airy nothing, stark belief? zoic art for as few as $600 US
My feigned insomnia lulls your mind to sleep, apiece or cheaper.
and what you call the power of assertion Get an imprisoned moth
is sheer manipulation of emotion. with the fossil bug of the month
at a whopping discount. They are as if alive, embalmed in the hard
sap of gymno- and angiosperms. This bright diaphanous cement,
100% all natural, is the only recipe, all else being trial and error.

ABOUT THE WATERFRONT

Dozing off into fried dreams,
dusks frittered
to bonne nuit, Skeltonic
rhododendrons within
and without the
telemorphokinesis,
Boston's vegetal forceps in bloom,
quagmires
of dactyloscopic rooks
on wires of air,
the tough tinsel nut
modernity
hung thriving
on the thread of
a generation. How much more
scintillantly splenetic
could the ragamuffins
of electronics become? Where
to cast or not to cast
downtown ellipses of joyhood
to trucks of passersby
behind the public gardens
in lanes of largesse
and others of fireproof
spring, strongbox
efflorescence,
securities jacked up,
life going hand in hand
with economics?
The sky coat is spread
wetly over the scrapers.
In the earth
ballistic bulbs burgeon.
The spade bank
is full of spades.
Piers are pincers.
They are paroles.
They are
sunk to their barrels,
filled with seagull-squashed
linen sleep and aquatic
projections into
the cobalt blotting sun.

PUSHKIN

Talking like Pushkin to his horse, I climb
into thick equestrian aesthetics. I'm
horseman and veterinarian in one
on an estate of troubled youth, I am
an aristocratic fop, hello,
galloping at full gallop shooting at treetops,
yahoo to you Sir in treble multiplication,
I know about stallions and I'm
out of here to the city soon, I must meet
N. or K., I forget which, and then the zisters C.
Sorry, I mean the sisters Z.
My sideburns incinerate the furniture in the salon
of Y. I do not care
for C++, for I live in the nineteenth century.
I barely lived through math at the Lycée.
I'm now dans une boutique.
Vous ne parlez pas français? Merde, vous êtes alors
crétin, mon vieux monsieur le barbecue!
What are you a Volga Tatar or something?
Actually I've never been to Kazan but I wanna go
some day, maybe when the emperor exiles me.
You look familiar, I know you from somewhere.
So what brings you to St. Petersburg on
this particular twist of the century?
Lozenges of the imagination climb
reflected in the Neva of the sky
and in the sky of the Neva and farther
along the Nevkas, and the stars, the stars
shine viscerally like old duel scars
anticipated. I am stuck at home.
I'll never see you, Paris, London, Rome.
Adrenal memory flows and gels and burns,
acting in combination with my sideburns.
I'll show you some transculture. Gospoda,
do you understand any Russian, ah?
Nyet? Damn, then I must speak to you in English.

CALCUTTA FLOWERS

for Shoumyo Dasgupta

The bard
addressing with his weightless quill
the human will
in its futility observes the florist
with bunched and garlanded conflorescences
who supplies his goods
to dozens of local cults
and is quite the worshipful man himself.
The sorry
samsara-swathed dusty sun
reemerges among the clouds
and the micromonsoon
wrung out of a nowhere pit
by Indra's unknowable hand
is over. Magic is the name of oblivion
and the reed pen
and flowers now
are merely methods of forgetting
even the unforgivable.
For the continuous self must forget itself
in time where everything reduces to its opposite
in the end and the end is merely the other
side of a fixed beginning. Here
the marigolds
in their January loveliness and buckets
on the sidewalk seem
to know their fate.
They silently belong to a caste; they are
on the wrong, the chantless
end of sacrifice. But here,
here in their flimsy present they
seem reconciled
to their route of migration. The sidewalk
enshrines many-handed anonymity.
This marigold was a poet long ago.

CRITICAL LEGAL STUDIES

We the thieves of all America,
pickpocket northerners, pinchbeck southerners,
eastern pilferers, western larceners,
Hawaiian nimmers, Alaskan hustlers
and the small outlying islands' cat burglars,
newsstand breakers, shoplifters, mall hoppers,
software pirates, con boys, con gals,
sporadic stealers, immigrant box snatchers,
Brit prigs, Canadian sneak sweepers, tongs,
kleptomaniacs of all stripes and affiliations
and credit card environmentalists,
the many and the few, gathered tonight in your brain,
demand the speedy expedition of our rights
as a self-constituted underpivileg. minority
in the claws and laws ("talons") of ("legit")
exploitation. A touch of analysis of reveals
the rhetorical construction of legal authority
in the tropes of an ideal model of justice. But
what is the essential core of a legal norm
but an ideality construed as a presence?
But what justice? Just this: a sphere of idealizations.
The next question we should ask is what
is the precise locus, the material receptacle
of this presence. This must, of course, be the letter
of the law. The spirit, then, abides in the letter.
But since an ideality can never be captured,
but at best tentatively indicated by the gross
materiality of the sign, it operates
in legal discourse in the form of a
trace, whose function is transcendent in that
it is bounded in a way that perforce relies on a
presumed metaphysics of presence. The espousement
of the grapheme rather than the phoneme
in establishing guilt, the pattern
of law should not be taken as evidence against,
but as rather a confirmation of our claim,
since the generally understood purpose
of counting the "dynamic" and "static" aspects of
imputability (given the indicia of a corpus
delicti) is consistent with the traditional
functions of the material sign vis à vis a presumptive
presence. It is therefore consistent (complicit, we
might say!) with the presumed primacy of speech

over writing (sound in letter as soul in body) that is
necessary to a metaphysics of justice (prejudice).
A sign denotes, de-notes, points to, a presence,
pre-sense, that is, that which precedes, pre-seeds,
its material expression in a language (land gwidge).
The sign, the grapheme, simulates but also contradicts,
negates (and thus, might we say, parodies) the ideal
structure that it implies. Therefore justice is at its core
a travesty of justice. How can we as a group
succeed in the absence of a "federal" funding scheme
to support ourselves as a minority of free agents?
Unionize or get powderized, get bowdlerized!
How can we be empowered if funds are not showered?
Answer your concerns in the affirmative,
the needs of your community. We request
that every cit, male or female, carry at any time 200%
of his/her one day's wages/salary/allowance/pension/per
diem or other income along with positive identification,
a small tax to pay for protection, available
to under-represented applicants in the government,
a useful function. Our justice is a sphere of practicalities.
We want development mentioned in the executive summary,
reckoned out to a need per crime basis,
well taken care of in the department of funds.

TABOO

things you can't mention are the insects
leaves of any kind of flora moral
also all the meta words like sense
trash grandparent non referent aberration
like electrocution of the invisible
broke cameraman cataclysms of the earth
imagine being born into him or her
oh and course I forgotten the snow
noshing these things trivialize everything
make you bank make you crank out nothing
2 bit sonnets on a tea afternoon
blokes laughing you in like
all those words are too regional
s well as other things you can't mention
haven't done itsy bitsy rock sunset
oldsmobile have no complaint
experience forget experience
the butterfly is a flying sandwich of pollen
the typewriter a typing sandwich of lying
of trying to speak the truth in language
snapdragons on the lawns
display their leonine yawns
the mind's verandah is clear
with its gardens of slats 2 silken
armchairs 2 bitter sockets of hope
doily what a flat woven pattern of
what you can't recognize can't mention
these things too are taboo in poetry

MY AEROFLOT

nights are like absence of focus in consciousness
but then you begin realize
which man consciousness & which not
of inner man in the man of inner self
which proclamations
which again dividing nuts airlines
which no dem& for under caking
simplicity as sign of remembrance
goat man drive s I become
fluent many language
fountainpen in fact of language
& God I always mean God
since I come
from my ethnic badground in Eastern Europe
& I make ye my own English
& I make ye mine type of English
& then some
b&its moon tuna
East European cuisine i.e.
vodka for breakfast on empty stomach
what does your furniture mean to my soul
my Slav root bag problems
& two three regurgitated stereotype
forget it
also to forget
bondage of grammar
which constrain true think
I no prob make myself underst&al
ladies & gentlemen
so now open
wh@ you see your left
2 fly bits of the friendly skies
recline your chair
magic opener of pilots drift
upward in the atmosphere of language yow
I'm taking you couple hundred lexemes higher
into stratosphere of we language

MODERNITY

for Ben Mazer

On route whatever, memory fails to serve,
blurred roses fling their mercenary blades
into the heart of placid driving. Death
flicks out a clear inaudible abrupt memento,
the noiselessness behind a splash of static,
and back at once to WZL rocking X,
and all is fine, and fresh, and half-fulfilled.
In some true sense there never was a Rome.
In some true sense there never is a home,
and in some truer sense there never will be.
(Two lines attributable to Kim Philby.)
The night has fallen. All barbecues are gone,
but stellar tylenol in dry handfuls pours
over the global villagers' collective nightmares.

A POLEMIC

I subvert by suggesting alternative forms of
to rely on outmoded conventions is highly problem
I subvert traditional notions of meaning
old structural approach challenged by a younger gen
binary oppositions pfut, zagging across the page
semantics of the visual sign can no longer be construed
simple tertiary relationship but rather
more complex more problematic seen outside a teleology
principle of the greatest reduction I now
am undermining a new body of readings
I mean ousside as a colloquial usage
but then again problem
but then again no problem
mindlobe how we undermine transparency
of language I "mean" how it get rid of this illusion
that we can see ideas of things through language
no matter how defamiliarize we its essentials
with usage of again technique
sense-trapping within compounds to the bunk
sense-chaining I believe the more appropriate word
just as maximally subverting meter
i.e. trying to write absolute prose absolute non-poetry
generates its own constraints own meter own poetry
evrbody shld try it sometime
or else as I was yesterday
subverting every syntactical
by suddenly telemomma existence as structured out
hangin three outflora gooters .
to specious and then I mean the sophists
are clearly underrepresented in the academy
have to try to hand out then
man I wanna subvert
something traditional language
is driving me nads spuds exploding
in the earth and then I salubriously reached the port
the bloodmaster suggested I wait a few minutes
till he apply his principles

so I waited 15 minutes in the well lit sauna
concresping with joy and redolence then the blurf
guardelia hit the switch and the who bhagla roared
splink splonk upon the carpet and I had
pfdno ek bawamnnnbh pevieg ba makmzinbb
erated over and over again as a sort of closure
abort abort how you hear me
do you copy again subvert subvert
and still meaning shines through
subvert it and still it shines through
that's the magic

A BLACK SQUARE, IN MEMORY OF KAZIMIR MALEVICH

Man is half-minded but two-handed. Some folks are obsessive wash-ers, some metempsychotically inclined, still others are watereaters. 18 misapprehends the involutional behavioristic phase, from which as if one observation would be to classify the ineffable as quasiexperience teen-laden & energetic. Often what is needed is not any sort of tenu-with parental authority, but the influence of a larger, correctly guided but essentially co-equal body of peers. It is their values that lilac top snow factually belligerent, it remains non-despotic, by rotating back-wards the pedal and resetting the counter to zero zero. For even such eloquent admission on the part of the national leaders remained unan-minished whereas prototypical interests are concerned, exempli gratia diagram corkscrew twisting into the firm plugging of vintage such as will not withhold from us tonight the appreciant morphonological lull spanning the hull into a singular void. From within, such unions are o' seventeen daily news and then sedentarily speaking there wasn't likely coiffed and not above a certain procedure across the street, under the their very nature electromagnetic. People are magnetized by ideas, as they are not free. There are waves even in stone. The centrifugal dust of earthonomics is crowding me out, but I tremble, vainly telling you to be staunch, to stand out against the clutter. Waves are in everythin Everything rumbles, but at its own frequency. Sporadically, cobalt co-lored dreams small indication steady, small indication that we are here

EQUALITY

the general consumer is cahooting in the mall
the general consumer is cahooting in the mall
the general consumer is cahooting in the mall
and his cellular is on

the manager in the parking lot has lunch today at three
the professor of divinity is lecturing abroad
the dental clinic's president has arranged to call you back
and his cellular is on

the coordinator's boyfriend flies a Boeing through the skies
his cellular is on and they are chatting as he flies
he promises her Paris cuz he knows some cheapo rides
and his cellular is on

LIZARDS

At close proximity,
from the middle of a noon-baked
dirt road permit me
to stare at the humans. I can see
a sun-distilled verandah and the steps
almost flaking away like a dream
into the heat.
The cacti stand in bloom.
Memory looms immobile.
From their great upstairs
they can see me too,
the humans. Why
am I attracted to their
society? I wouldn't dare
come closer
to the keepers of that hearth.
I hear Ms. Understanding
chattering on the cellular,
rattling good conversation. The samovar
is all a-go, she permits
herself a cup. And I,
what do I matter to her, a sorry
reptilian? The praying
mantis on my mind is food. This morning's
glory gets to me. We are lizards,
featherless quadrupeds.
Objective reality
is not unlike ourselves, and we
are multiple writhing selves
in a lizard-structured world.

A SONNET IN C

My dear printf, I never saw you skip
a newline when you found one in a file.
A non null pointer plugged into our while
loop } else if { as if, printf, to tip
the computational balance of my heart,
my file, my life, my method - and then some.
But how much memory, malloc'ed for their sum,
supplies me with this ability to insert
another leaf into a binary subtree of
log n complexity in one long thought,
which is not bad for huffy humans? God,
herein we input ardor of our love
and output selfless structs like battle shields
in your name in our spacious data fields.

HELLO TO GORBACHEV

Anent, ex-president, your cracking down
big time on drunkenness in Russia where
your reverie bloomed in and on the air
in 85: dissent in every town
was mounting fast. Many in silent wrath
turned out fierce moonshine in domestic stills,
while those without the high-tech rig and skills
reached satisfaction by a simpler path.
Water, yeast, sugar, fruit, a glass jar and
a latex glove held by a rubber band
over the jar's round mouth: just when the brew
was ripe, the flaccid glove filled out anew,
rising on vapors - a saluting hand.
We joked that this was our hello to you.

ERGO

for Harriet Zinnes

Lethe me tomorrow if I can train so
                    actly
tyking the moist canopy
Mass betake
                         mistfossicking
minstrel on the road
cleverer do
unraveling the migrant mod
            a stock of lilies
again with
              saltpeter
                         pepperpiper
radiotelepisty
                    bravo bravo
                              again
with now and later
with always now and later
never
in the root square of the ego
with ago

A LANGUAGE HAREM

First with twenty tea bags, then changing hands,
"ideal gift for your family and friends,"
the pink box of Bigelow Red Raspberry Tea,
confirming its printed claim, had come to me
handy and empty. It now held flashcards
all covered with a host of Hindi words
penned lovingly in Devanagari script in
my own, then as yet tentative, handwriting.
Perfectly fitting into its pink length,
some cards lay down while some stood in full strength.
There was a method to their distribution.
Each card was like a gold-embroidered cushion,
and every word was like a queen of hearts.
I would spend hours delving into the cards.

DUSK RAGA

for Andy McCord

Just as the lonely, wicked, wild and glad
eyes know and do not know by letting drop
in every detail of their daily dread
the flowering and rainfall and mishap
of birth, there's a benignness comes about
the streets. Well-lined eyelashes flutter by
like Kali's black bewildering butterfly
and life is tantra to the marrow, but
I do not know myself. The slow and fast
warm intersections squirm with liquid ease,
melt away. The gods cannot undo the past.
But I'll refrain from feigning expertise.
Past bougainvillaeas, samsara's saris float
lighter than magic in my tragic dreams.
My heart has killed a goat at Kalighat.
At nightfall, the world isn't what it seems.
Vague autorickshaws hooting out of sight
and back, I pause to stare at life at these
bedraggled corners in the red-light night,
but will refrain from feigning expertise.
All day, eyes in their speaking sparkling millions
find mine, but at dusk differences are
less clear, voices more similar, dark darshans
finally over. No one can tell I'm near.
The flower-shop shut, my bidi crushed, I hide
in sultry shadows. The question of a star
shines through the smog. These people understand
I'm somewhere but don't know exactly where.
And I, I could not help them if they asked.
The faster beats the heart. So fast. So fast.

TYPING YOGA

I once needed some lecture notes typed up,
scrawled on a cheap gray writing-pad
with some silly lotus-shaped logo in the corner
for the embellishment of the page. For the umpteenth
time I was ordering myself to be better organized,
to be more systematic with my data.
So I went to a Calcutta street typist,
seated with an ancient-looking typewriter
at a minute table beside a vendor
of green coconuts. To my great surprise
reading my undisciplined writing was a breeze
for him. He touch-types at Rs. 2 per page,
fast, few typos, while the other man opens me a coconut,
chopping the top off with a crooked cleaver,
and there's no additional charge for a straw.
The heat is benign today, but the sun
shines too brightly on the sidewalk,
it's hard to hide your eyes from it. Autorickshaws
sail honking by, bus personnel drones *cholo*,
cholo, cholo, let's go, folks, let's go! But I stay
and sip while the typist types
and talks about his brother. He says,
"He is a writer like you also. Writes many many poetries
in Bangla. No good in my opinion. Nobody publish."
Characters did jumping jacks on the page
like warming-up karatekas speeding up
into kicks. Kia! Kia! Kia! Kia! Very fast. Each of his fingers
had a black belt in punching out lines. Amid overpopulations,
where labor is so poignantly cheap,
you survive only by perfecting your skills.

MY INTERNATIONAL

I'm a Jewish New Yorker from America.
I come from a background of my family,
mostly from Brooklyn,
with a touch of Lower East Side.
I have three golden dental teeth in my mouth,
a silver one and a gold one. My grandmother
came from Bukhara in the nineteenth century.
She had the custom
of keeping a Bukharan cook in residence.
A female cook.
Both quickly picked up that Yankee
habit of smoking self-rolled cigarettes,
or smokes. Something
they would never have done in Bukhara. OK,
I'm not exactly sure what I'm saying.
OK, maybe, I dunno, maybe I'm Russian.
Yeah, maybe I'm that Russian
from Wicked Walnut Wool Street (Ave.)
in Cambridge, Mass.,
or something that resembles him or her
in absent-mindedness and peculiar manners
of speech. Maybe that. Maybe I smoke
crude cigarettes, 2 packs daily,
ripping off the filters, drinking three
Dublin boys under the table.
Or maybe I'm a German biochem
grad student who laughs at American PC,
soaking white teeth in purple Pinot Noir. I am Greek.
I am Latin. I am Chinese. I am Hindustani.
Hello? Hello? Where is my national identity?
Who cares? Why would anyone care?
These are my clothes, take them.
These days everything is international.

MY AUSTRALIAN POETS

Dear friends, my Australian poets,
from the face of the Russian friendly people
I offer to present you this poem,
because in the heart I feel an urge to address you.
We in Russia believe in fraternity of poets/
sorority of poets.
Sorry, mate, that's not actually true,
but I just had to say it.
Vodka is only pretext,
grass is only pretext
and this glass is only pretext,
howeverly, this my Russian heart
is not pretext
to envelop you with my internal,
but as a means. Manifesto
is for man/woman of yesterday.
For man/woman of tomorrow
is my marrow,
is the devil's dozen,
as we say in Russia,
of just hello.
Under the people, over the people
and under the people
spins marsupial hope,
spikes polar bear understanding.
My hug to you
is not misunderstandable.
Suppose we had not
the means of communication, then
you would just look past me
at the creaky land crabs,
combusting coconuts
and keeping your poems to yourselves.
But I know the English,
and here I am digging you,
and here you are digging me,
my mother would not let me go,
my father would not let me play
without the English.
My most magical mates,
thank you for drinking a winter of words
to my summer of love.

FOUND SONNET

Glade Powder Fresh™ is a delicate
light fragrance that instantly freshens the air
with the soft scent of talc. Use Glade anywhere
in the home to effectively eliminate

odors. Glade freshens the air while leaving a light
clean scent throughout your home.
Shake well before each use; hold can upright;
press button and spray toward center of the room.

Do not set on stove or
radiator or keep where
temperature

will exceed 120° F, as container
may burst. Do not puncture
or throw in fire.

IN RE THE DEATH OF THE AUTHOR 2

"The imaginary is as real as the real."

Mellow, declarative arbitration of
and management of my ropy life affairs
in academic poverty abrades
the will to resolution. And so?
Moi, je ne longer care.
And as regards the literary sphere,
it too is more like a funnel than a globe.
I am, dear colleagues, no fop.
Fresh mayo be upon
your non-Euclidean iconoclastic clamp-on
credentials. Boy,
this book is giving me ideers. If only
this silver autumn I could orchestrate
my brave escape from here
into another sphere,
if only I could silence this parade
of decadence into a more winged bender
inside this lucid gender-blender.
Where are all binary oppositions gone?

There comes a day your life goes to the john
and never comes back. Smoke of factories
in eructating air thickens. The young
umbrellas still bloom full of expectation.
The heap of days lies multiplied by one.
According to your essays and your stories,
you'd seen the twitchy, twitchy side of things
among the hiccupping magnolias once
back in your many days as academic
way off the tenure track in a state of
underdress. Tremulously
a radical conception in the literature
becomes, then unbecomes a revolution.
Your hands which once clasped the keyboard lie
unnerved in the dispersal of your impact.
Everything gets inverted. Bye,
the sweetest bread critical tongues can buy.
Bye-bye, the tenure track! Bye, MLA!
They're turning into chimney folks.
I am ontologically telling you,
this is yours, this is the real death of the author,
dearest colleague.

CIVILIZATION

The oxen and the barns behind the prison
walls and the pond come audibly alive.
There is a village here in shifty weather.
The priest emits a cough in point of season;
weary of villagers, he would much rather
socialize with the gaol-birds. It is 1775.

Of all our lots this isn't yet the saddest,
for no one prefers the noose to the stick.
Or is it 1866, and sold
mud-cheap? And from the city arrives the realist artist
to paint his sad reminders to the world
where souls in pain file out to do their works.

Or is it 1994, and does
the rain lash down with special aggravation
across the medium security
into two hundred half-transparent windows?
The superintendent wears his car and duty
compliments of the Department of Correction,

asks a few questions of his visitors,
a delegation of international criminal lawyers
looking into the American experience
who braved foul weather for instructive cause.
What they see here translates them into trance,
as their the leader of the delegation utters.

Or is this God knows when - and the mixed wood,
meaningless, looms before my hopeless eye?
And does the dogs' bark entertain the chasers?
All suddenly darkens, darkens. Death is good.
I've lost my chance in the ferns, prepared to die,
yet wish I were among the prisoners.

Dawn on the sundial, crepuscularly rich
light breaks over the svelte
shrine steeple where they drag me through the suburbs.
Which human murdered which?
Looking up from their coffee and kebabs,
citizens scowl at me - a blur-eyed belt.

I could be mad, knowing how madness flings
its dice, paves with intentions roads to hell,
how veins explode with listlessness and languor.
Ah catch that something in the mind that clings
and tingles, as remarked by Schopenhauer,
and prods and subjugates, and drives the will.

But likewise they who in each goddamn city
with an apparent dignity walk the streets
or hospitals of their general at-largeness
in lifelong convalescence from nativity
hold in their skulls no liberated essence,
whom evanescence tempts with chaster sweets.

While Jeremy Bentham's head sneezes in London
with echoes through the hallways of his University,
it rains on jail roofs all over Massachusetts.
The delegation exits the prison library, the superintendent
signs the Dept. of Correction's gift navy blue baseball hats,
smiles enlightened ethnocultural diversity.

The priest has left the chapel. White haze on all
(whose meaning whispers all men are unfree,
reductio ad absurdum, freedom is death),
my young, imprisoned, lying and lifer soul
has chosen life and prison and physical breath
by whose decrees no truth can set it free.

LIGHTS OUT

I have nothing really to confess
How can you disbelieve me on this one
The lights are almost out no one waits
For me now even you sleep
Why come home at all
I should have stayed
Macking on ghosts on the sidewalk
Under bolts of lightning but no rain
The meaning of life is empty
Our words are how we fill time
I stumble on a whirring fan in the dark
Grab by the throat
The bottleneck of my drear

DOING

So how are you there then
how there you been this again
how you are I mean how are you
I'm fine fine thank you man
I'm fine thank you man I'm fine
I have mastered the science of desire
and since then I'm always fine
I have mastered the lingo of desire
and since always doing fine
I've mastered the sillies and
missiles of misapprehension
and have always thence been fine
and you yourself man how are you doing
yourself I'm fine too thank you man
where did ya say ya been
chicago chicago man
chicago man gettoutta here
gettoutta here man tha's some place to go
yow actually I usually
been Chicago coupla times myself I telling you
gone there a coupla times myself n you
how you say you been doing
told ya fine man I always fine
ever since I
mastered me dialing of sports live fashion
how art thou fine too
but my gnosticism is getting way to me
awaking me amidships the night
ploughing me home through the ken sphere
so how did you say you were doing
okay I'm doing okay thank you man
this kennisphere this is kennisphere of mine
ever since discover
how to open on left side
I alwayswalways been doin beaucoup de fine
cuz I'm's evolving
and you can't already see my toes
turning inward
and from there we can take it any distance
whichever can do it by itself
it always replies the same
and yourself man how
how bet ya been doin yourself?

NOTHING

I never tried it with a whore
(tho done sick shit with
a cooperating partner
and seen whorenography and hornography)
but here I am
at 36 on the Singel Canal
in Amsterdam,
undertheinfluencing on foot
down the straat -
and you will please excuse me,
but I am intoxicated.
Beautiful & exposed
professionally
she is seventeen y.o.
or so, equivalent in Euros. I
am looking for a bathroom,
have nothing to say to her
except sorry.

ART

myyoungeredbodyhungered
helplesslytimeandtimeagain
spikedwithaliketwohundred
telepathicthoughtsofstrain
lostintheirownplainleisure
inmyownkindofmindmeasure
noopticalillusionbut
realityfleshandbuttIsay
chaquejourchaquepensée
washedinmybloodismut
teringmutteringthese
cretsofmyfuturepastandjoy
settingupmodelsofadecoy
concrescentblossomingsof
thelipsthelapsbecomingsof
terandsofterinthemistoflife
inthestarkclarityofmybelief

DEATH OF A POET

Once there was a poet who thought
poetry was just syntax, blah-blah,
just style and no life or death related
content. He once wrote, "God has no
guts!" He wrote it plain for effect, as
he was no believer in the afterlife or
in God and fancied himself a tough
stylist and no mystic. Well, he was
plumb wrong about all that. When he
dead, God grab him by the skin of his
face and He ask, "Who have no guts,
Yablonski? Who was you trying to
insult down there? I'll show you guts,
God dammit." And He revive
Yablonski's flesh and He put his soul
back in the decrepit stinko flesh and
He bang bang bang the poor bastard
against the wall like a whale
against the rocks with his bare hands
till Yablonski's all blue chin, calf and
asshole. Now, now, don't worry.
Put your mind at ease.
This is Massachusetts.
Relax, it's just a story.

OUTSKIRT

rooks loudly successive on the wire
transmit the forecast
concrete will be whitewashed
citizens are advised against leaving trash
behind dumpsters
overfilled but try to hurl on top instead
easier to load
into garbageman's vehicle
keeps coons out too
then there's like a ramp going down
into the no park area
don't even think about it
the tow truck dude
will fleck your brow with grief
if you catch his crowbar drift
his coveralls hang
funny as you walk through
there are precautions everywhere
on playgrounds gone to seed
on hydrants obliterated
with graffiti of youth
with graffiti of philosophy
down to the waterfront
an industrial door
reveals a tender lining
of darkness and the clattering smell
of a work process
sans attempting
to understand you must abandon the premises
immediately
you are not welcome
nobody says that but the safety
rules on the wall suggest you leave
the rooks again
like flying garbage settle on the sidewalk

HISTORY

To a cuckoo tone in the tangled
brush among the living,
your heart forgiving,
active, new-fangled,

go back to the rainy season
where the wigwams stand alive,
dew-freshened. We have
traveled into their vision.

The day, run dry for our good,
has joined paths with man
in potterings about the wood
like a well-watered raccoon.

The red moon and bonfire,
pipe, rifle, the wild
forest's wailing child
at night possess the air.

Not daring to describe
our poisoned future
under cover of nature
the shaman flees the tribe.

He's seen the lot of our men,
his eyeball albumen
is shot through with red
unmitigated dread.

NOT REALLY FAMILIAR

preternatural groaning
        deep layer clepsydra
same bed hose doting
        departing dry
have you not limbered
        dim lit calendars
subordinated only
        catapulted scarface
seventeen drove
        now skull duskfall
hapless caravans
        barns of the noble
conditions whipbird garage
        wish man in trellis
middle class ounces
        middle claw inches
tables of depletion
        cellular stitches
gastroenterology
        uvular lurches
bitter snack mismanagement
        dirigible churches
into plummeting above
        home diddle gotcha
absolved absolutely nakedly
        brink clam Bogota
majority verity
        sand talk on sand
masterful ablations
        partisan absconding
hoop cut in on long
        island barber get
out pleat continues
        with determination
we have never been a part
        of so called alternative
us into that category
        highly problematic
it just seems to be
        natural progression
doing what we do best
        not really familiar

JOB PROSPECTS

When out of left and out of right
came dreams and whipped us with their might
on the high seas of treason
like mangoes out of season,

as we were going from here to there,
as we were going left to right,
because I usually like to wear
some kitchenware, some tableware

and some salmon cologne.
I spray it on.
My underwater underwear,
transparent to the world around it,

gleams. What could I more desire?
I have the manners and the bite,
a couple of loose hands for hire
and half a crate of dynamite.

CERTAINTIES

There are certainties that will reach you soon,
which are seldom evident from the start.
Meanwhile semi-meanderingly Boston
flows like magic into the empty heart,

lends a vacant hand. Frost bites off, glues on
fingernails on the bronze of giants
while a local bank shuts off with a block
the accounts of delinquent clients.

Cars advance. There is nothing to stem the flow
of pedestrian stars and celestial eyes.
Simply follow suit through a neon glow
over glaring blackenings of the ice,

but be careful just as you are alone.
An experience nothing can beat will pass,
milling neon bone to neon dust,
sweeping neon pearls through dusk neon.

Christmas nears with a vengeance: its jingling bell
like a tinkling lily in gelid fluff
overhangs the premises where they sell
alcoholic beverages and stuff.

Quickened social life as a form of art
lets all things drop into a woven waltz.
Feeling sorry for tramps and bums, the heart
is again recounting its idiot pulse

and advancing into the crowd. "Go home,"
whisper cabs in their yellow checkered fuss.
Early Santa, his whiskers suffused with rum,
whispers softly, whispers, and whispers thus:

"Everything impels one to reaffirm
that inevitably there comes a time
when it's time to tighten your grip on life
in a grim suspension of disbelief."

AN ANTIQUE MODERN COOL FOR T. S. ELIOT

Middling to mesmerizing
Mediterranean breeze.
Minstrelsy in the echoes
of the heart's bell tower.
Refractory angst gullible
Elviswise, of Cinderella:
watch it man gratuitously
the unmannable meringue.
Metanondescriminasturbation
is the buzz word of the day
if you're really smart
and, like me, into culture.
Intellectuals engage semi-intellectuals
in no end of hesitation waltzes.
Destabilization filters the lowly
proximate ends of finality
across coexistent tonality
into the sphere of my mind's palm.

Day in, day out,
Maxim Hugh Gorky Jr., Crystal Clerics Inc.,
the familial context mistaken at face value,
certain powerful embellishments of hair style,
hair today and hair tomorrow, and hair beyond,
Hot Water Supplier General,
Hot Water Supplier Particular,
Street, Park Area and Sidewalk Water Supplier,
Boris Yeltsin Godunov Boyscout Bisque Special,
Burger King's Cheese Double Decker Whopper Deal
Du Jour, toujours with extra large fries to go,
a raincoat and an umbrella, wicker, handburger,
eyeburger, lipburger, brainburger, mindburger,
Ye Caravans of High Hope and Other Stories,
your punch-drunk buddy waxing vicepresidential,
Social Stigma and Sons, classes by themselves,
current croutons and earlier croutons,
borscht, bullshit and casserole of your choice,
the madame who welshed and her male accomplices,
faint vacillating administrations
in a web of stark financial disaster,
whispering property rights
in the teeth of a shrinking securities market,
an ever-expanding set of opportunities,

a never-ending stream of opportunities,
Hick Yam Cutler Waits, his impact on drama,
his impact upon the imaginative self,
his impact upon himself and his tough
almost complete aura of guru and god,
mayo, papa, this newsletter and the binoculars,
rain, tinfoil, malt, amber and patterned dreams,
their communistic implications,
Jacques Derrida, critical legal studies,
the serpents of oblivion, their crawling ways,
their tarnished, varnished, crushed, soft
distinguishing marks, unpardonable locutions,
the silence of locusts in a valley,
cellos with arms like statues', a twang of sitar,
flowers reminiscent of demons and little else,
flowers reminiscent of demons in little vases,
a fragrance reminiscent of nothing in particular,
as also your goblet's intrinsic sparkle,
myself, eighteen elephantine trunks,
and, needless to say, the swift
familiar deer of Alaska,
all approached without prejudice
and with an OK frame of reference,
are decidedly damnngam cool!
Each a stroke of nothing but genius.

Emparloured ladies pay their debt
to the late T. S. Eliot.

Frolicky like kroliki,
they warble thus: You listen to us -
for most everybody digs this;
for he who wagers all, conquers everything;
for every cool rover should know
that we'll stand behind him, I guess;
and/or know that we'll help clean up his mess;
for we are the ladies at Bonus Plus;
just call us. They drive me nuts. Anyways.
Stay cool, Tom S.E., write soon! They sing:
Subcult is a great sub
sonuvabitch, - to which I most gladly subscribe -
Yrs eminently postmodern
and deadly, Philip Nikolayev

MIDLIFE

My kettle finitely boiling, I recover
from reverie. The windows after the shower
stand brightened, and the barricades of books
on the floor arch their philosophic backs,
bare their teeth. Unanswered mail piles. Coffee's ready.
Capitalist society is greedy,
monthly bills like moth larvae eat my checks.
Small print hides multitudes of clever tricks
in valued customer junk mail. Tunes
are rife on local radio. Life continues
as conscience aches. Where is my freedom, where?
It's night. The sky spreads stellar solitaire.
The Milky Way yawns watching from on high
cities where young ambitions come to die.

IN RE THE DEATH OF THE AUTHOR

As I hear say on the cellular grapevine these days
wishful thinking whatever, but as I was saying
comes again and forgets you as I was
suggesting, leaves disobeying, mumbling
to himself, whom he calls poet except of necessity
unshaven, idiot, always fiddles with doorknobs
taking off real slow and then gaining velocity,
knowing not which way the heart's habit throbs,
but real smart fellow, look what he's got
and killed indefinite times over, not
to mention a thousand times insolvently inspired,
striking root in your thoughts inkling by inkling.
The modern critics have long proclaimed him dead.
Dim bulbs think they can deconstruct everything.

CAMBRIDGE AT SNOW

Come, February, evicting through our windows,
hoarfrosted over with a Rousseau jungle scene
(a white and white little-known version, too),
with chilly lions sprung to life, chasing
the lackluster reminiscences of room comfort
away into the epistemic night
with a relentless Massachusetts harshness. Officially
external navigation ends in the showcased snowstorm
whose quicksilver-slinging tentacles and aplomb
enmesh every square inch of a pitfall-filled sidewalk.
Yet I must go, love, I must venture outdoors and catch
the rigors of Charles River in its raw abandonment
and pride, measured out to hallucinatory imprecision.
I must go and explore the bridges
besmeared with an ashen moonlight and remark
a snow-swamped, streetlamp-looted pandemonium
confronting the First Church and abnegating
the Commons into a stewardship of stripes of destruction.
But a new synthesis is already being adumbrated
by the rollicking present. I must
bring home the groceries! Tomorrow
vagaries of the climate will be mentioned more than once
yet little understood by the local intelligentsia,
agreeable, swapping jokes and generally bent
on freeing their motor vehicles
from under hefty drifts of soft predicament.

AMERICAN FARMERS VISIT A RUSSIAN COLLECTIVE FARM

oh how madly how verdantly flamboyant
yanks came hardening with bottles of rum
and how we all rolled to nowhere
for hours as one ball
fraternizing through rough conversation
as cultural exchange
and then flam bam in comes the moment
of sparse generosity unleashed
tangentially upon a garden of sham
sheep as they clamber
out of their own silhouettes
s'as to raise another
through a silk in the sky
to us the human mowers
and this now a different place
with a different people
and to gain velocity here is not again
problematic because
the sheep are as against the section cars
and the section cars are as against the cattle
as one to three
cool bovine quadrupeds
and then hip zip take me out of here
to the nearest brickhouse
so I can hiccup
and hold me under water
for a few minutes
but make sure I can fill my lungs with air
or else you'll drown me

A COMPLEX OBJECT

butter tatter telephone wrinkle
guttersnipe periwinkle broadsheet gelding
boomer encapsulation stubble gut
funeral apple shower surd
debt tickle whisper toy
caprice visitant pill pumpernickel
swath footstep interpenetration spine
bottle chap exit wad
vertigo belittling caterpillar corpse
cognizance upkeep telepathy oilcloth
hibernation ligament polliwog friend
title centigrade scumbag price
plasticity Elysium steppe fox
recognition archeology ballbearing mud
larrikin function noun entry
etymology origin datum 1868
adjective workingman expression Atlantic
boomer settlers area bridge
builder gall mite plant
life zip manner puffer
moon shell family Naticidae
clobber form blowfish globefish
Tetraodontiformes screw thread hydro
phial hissy thermostat South
Euclid population 23866 lawns
lift loft century transition
rank condition rate amount
end blockade root crop
fingerprint nut transplant mortgage
ground obligation aircraft surface
lifer boost chair vacuum
element suddenness volvox attack
leg cargo implication train
crate push brother fence
pondweed shadecloth specification system
fan selection humidity growth
comfort arse gear speed
bathroom yacht widow nightjar
US operetta 1905 corset
chook dive tab flap
control device loop remnant
appendage reorganization projection card
use aid file insert

border garment airfoil hinged
surveillance bill cost program
tabulator typewriter data column
metal tab can container
band army model designation
stump force landing names
eight maker receiver birth
money photo home page
reconnaissance shadow breath male
esprit trusting alert beer
area atheist foxhole discotheque
Paris whirl thole gunwale
boat side fullness atomizer
automaker kaon snowshoe bar
cockchafer melolontha vegetation adult
boletus hallway shotgun thread
variation shack York granny
elixir restroom public John
summer bear mama structure
law window shaft floor
middle air context hill

SOUP

ed
id Rog
ody née
there is w
eat it which

elling soup,
meal-save o
littlele confectio
trendlette, experts
ly Soup appeared t
the concept, but th
it. It all began with
, who has been sellin
or years from Soup K
ational, his stand on
eet. His churlish dem
s must move like
he left after orderin
r wrath) pas parodie
ode courted the ire o
ut made his yum
more popular. And s

gh profile of soup-
ly Soup, which star
n store and now
ines formed out
uld not be enou
y, vegetable
se. The chai
tores at a b
oblems ensu
nded too q
gel, a pa
utive o
8 of t

m

A CABLE TO HAWAII

Reveal to me your sunny mystery,
oh beautiful state of Hawaii,

land where obligations are zero,
like teeth in the mouth of an armadillo!

Hand me a roll of pinup pix,
let my soul fly through human tropics,

let the feet do their stuff,
cut the crap! 'Nuff

said. Let's open our lips
and inhale topless tulips

taken sensuously by the hand,
led appetizingly over warm sand.

I'm into music before everything,
for which I dig the empyrean,

dancing more freely thru the air
than the whitehot tips of local girls' hair.

Work is bullshit. I'm pau.
Let's hele with the muumuus to the luau.

IMMINENT TOWN

The vinegar sun of November, stiffly unmediterranean here,
is cloudy and sour on the subject of our arrival. You drive,
I gaze and then no longer gaze at the sunset, but at times
the free course of my reverie halts, and the world heaves
back down into focus, revealing a time and place in acute
elongation and the fluidity of all road-swallowed existence.
Coins pile gaily from pockets into collection gadgets
as we plough a motley landscape to its timely solution
across cloverleaf highfalutions of the highway, wheeling
east of everything, with dips into lilac oblivion. Shaken
gently awake, I chuckle to discern a lovelorn and weary
glittering baby Manhattan from Tappan Zee Bridge - a must see
still, about to be developed. A kiss away, a clear future
suggests itself promptly, waving at us its little flags: New
York. In minutes, life will be a stark matter of crossroads.

AN OCCASIONAL SIGHT

Past the broad rosebush where the sun professors
over some vacant benches on the lawn,
he daily walks alone, a sad emeritus,
seemingly out of sorts, bright glasses on,
with high reservedness in place. His place,
three storeys tall, is down five blocks from here,
from where - just plug your ears and shut your eyes -
you'll smell the midnight ride of Paul Revere.
Nice house. You'll be surprised that men so dry
inhabit solitudes so vast. The play
of light on stained glass captures to perfection
the chlorine discipline of a private hell
some of his colleagues understand so well.
That which fully commands his whole affection.

FROST REMINISCES ON DOING FARMING JUST NORTH OF BOSTON

Frank shows up mornings every once awhile
with certain kinds of service or delivery.
"Who goes there?" - "Bob, I brought your fertilizer.
I missed our pranks the time I was away." -
"Oh, thank you, Frank. I missed ya too, old bud.
How much ya got there?" - "Seven hundred pounds." -
"A sizable amount. I'm so obliged." -
"Don't mention it, it's fair for your good money." -
"One hopes." - "But I'm plain positive it's true." -
"Now, here's the pay." - "Amen, I feel rewarded."
Our hands we shake, our morning faces shine
with satisfaction from a warm transaction.
He thinks, poets are wicked generous with their purse.
I say, good neighbors make good fertilizer.

FROST *INTERVIEWED BY* THE BOSTON FARMER

I been farming, like the legend says,
several years in this area. In farming all
depends on sober calculation. What you get
is what you sow (plus under what circumstances,
plus how you do it). There will be variations.
If you time right the moment for sowing, e.g.,
you can enhance your output by a high margin. Let's see,
I'm looking at how for years now I always been able
to hit bumper yields in my best years
and to get nice results even in my piece o' shit years
by just timing the sowing process right. With this method,
will others succeed? You betcha! Which is why
I got up to speed myself. Capitalism got me
right where I am. What will be the next question, mister?

MR. GOD:

Your unrecognition of our desire
has been horrible, as we've all been desirin
and desirin and desirin it for years, admirin
your notional authority in its sparse attire
of sanctimonious communicativeness,
our proletarian origins notwithstickin,
desirin, cravin, ravin, kith and kin
preservin, havin nada to confess
about nuttin bad. Small, medium or large
sprite, coke on tap or bottled pepsi? Gotcha.
I much enjoy work out in paradise.
They pay me well up here. The tips are large.
But mister, how about lettin me watch ya
transform them academics into mice?

BOHEMIAN BLUES

The cold March afternoon waxed languid
with its late hours. The cinders sang
their lowpitched ancient fireplace ditty
with an insufferable hang.

I wasn't sleepy. On the table
there sat potato chips galore
with Morellino de Scansano,
vintage of 1994.

Fingers of shadow played obscurely
behind the weakened flames. Blasé,
the Christmas cactus nodded mildly
like an art dealer from LA.

And I, with no premeditation,
returned the Shelley to the shelf,
unwound sublimely on the sofa,
lit up a cig and shot myself.

TALKING DIRTY

My dick swells up like a silver spoon in heaven.
The angels and archangels will easily recognize my dick,
that elegant utensil reaching for its sugar basin,
where it belongs. My love will pardon me talking dirty!
It's just that I am convinced that poetry can exist
at any level because it is absolute and pure.
Swear words are perpetually Elizabethan. Forsooth,
they hang in mellow clusters. Have I or have I not
this welcome transgression made into your pussy,
my soulful boner communicating fertility? Naturally,
I have. And now I, doting on your skin and moaning
and beloving your tits, know I'm soon going to squirt
and like to hold off a while with metaphors, as I'm not
technically even talking dirty, just telling it like it is.

DEGRAMMAR

Amicably, trebly
deflog, degrammar.
Alors, we say have'd
wha we have'd
ego alpho na care
wha go before,
wha go in the past,
negotiant, lousy
Velcro stupa. No,
no have to yet.
Yep, you have to.
Yuppers, have to br
other. The. Have to,
yuppers, have to,
brother the other.
Brother the The.
The zebra of Brazil,
of Buenos Aires, am. He
have to almost claim
Arabian descent
in language, mais oui.
Yet Euro kinda, out
of here. Degrammar.
Diagram mango flap,
logauditorium.
Up to, lap to, have to.
Up to, lap to, have to.
Mo, Moe Modality
tinker load
Girolamo ergo
Don't have to, Savo
narola, He. So Him
happen. Mon.
Let Him, Is.
Always logograph
unremember
immortality, arts. Atr-
abilious temperament,
have to, Last.
Am here to venge Ya.
Am always, a. Him, It.
At new era come
and from here
go new direction.

AGNOSTICISM

Why is it so mellow?
Why is it so quiet?
I confess that I dunno,
tho it must be my diet.

How so?
Dunno.
Why, do
you? No.

Hey, mister, wait,
take the 68.
Yeah? Where does that go?
Dunno.

Ahoy, tell me, boy,
who was Frida Kahlo?
Wish I knew, but dunno.
To pretend seems callow.

I have found in Central Park
the remains of Noah's Ark.
But I ask you, who is Noah?
I admit that I dunno.

"Y'all so yellow, hollow winds,"
I'll trill a capella.
Oh la la, why so, how so?
I decidedly dunno.

Buddy, ask me something.
Ask me anything.
For instance, is this my
tuxedo. Dunno, why?

THE TEMPO

India, into your heart
I take the red artery of a road.

Hurrah for the country route
where no buses ply. Now what?

To such parts one may go
by a big scooter-like thing called "tempo."

The driver sets the bakshish,
how much per each in cash.

The earth road is washed out with rain,
atypical for this season.

A buffalo in the red evening mud
stares at me like I'm stark mad.

The beat tempo trundles off fast,
crammed through the roof, thrusts

past the small town's farthest
end and continues

down along the Jamuna
under a whole lemon moon.

Through the last drops of twilight
we ride and toot into the night,

and at an obscure junction
some kids flag us down and jump on.

Way over capacity, they ride
hanging on the outside.

Collectively headlightless in the pitch dark,
awash, squeezed and jolted in the engine's work,

and nobody can see the rut!
What if we run into a mud hut?

They say Lord Krishna's hand keep you safe
and keeps the peacocks asleep

in every ashrams garden.
The river turtles beam back at the moon.

Everybody dreams of food,
even effigies of wood.

In 50 minutes we'll hit the hamlet
where I'm staying the night.

I will alight.
The tempo will go.

I'm alone. The stars shine huge
on the universal mirage.

MATINS

for Subhas Mukhopadhyay

The vulture's circle
is presently complete over a knot
of sundry awakened vagrants
and human transport trapped in the bluish fog
of a blaring progress
rising on the thick tall eyebrows of Gariahat
with meditative precision to its daily unfreedom.
Calcutta in her February flowering
vine-tangled flows into focus.

Up early too
I find many options on the sidewalk:
drink sugar-cane pulp,
get your ears cleaned out, or stubble shaved off
street style to a baby shine
with a touch of cool lapis,
with a minor perfection
you could never accomplish by yourself.

I will sip warm
masala tea, play
a swift game of carom
with the tea man's boy,
perched under the city's hungry goddess
sticking out at me her tongue of flame
from the bottomless coalpit of her presence.
Guess whose side she is on in this battle!
The boy's father overcharges me two rupees
but tho' I'm broke
I uncharacteristically refuse to haggle.

Like a telescope reversed into a microscope,
I begin to notice the smallness of things
after a long mouthful of betel,
with a smoldering rope igniting
my Charminar filterless,
walking like your pensive Marxist professor,
but so lost in thought
even the honking of civilization fails to get my attention.

A million poets have lived here,
small and big,
the singing of their lungs
lush on the air.
I can hear them and they
can hear my silence, the experience
of joy as pain, which comes with age,
which always comes too soon.

A FORTUNE

Damn nice restaurant, you think,
this could be Harvard, all Western grub,
Euro-like and also the style,
the chef eager to befriend you,
Italian diploma, they
undertake party orders,
think apricots, poker, aperitif,
flowers in trendy crackleware,
but this is New Delhi, also think
neat filings in the file cabinet,
big glass-ball paperweights
on the minister's table,
all in the nature of being
passably well organized and belonging
to some pretty nice clubs,
caste, configuration of stars, wearing
the stones your mom's astrologer
prescribes, the rest, along with sparkling
expectations, comes natural to
a hereditary young millionaire
not without religious feelings and
with a whale of a future in the light
industry, you think, hurrah for the Brits
who invented the colonial style,
you know it's all coming to you,
and yes, the yacht, fellow Rotarians
will excuse your French, but you know, also,
how to wear your dhoti, and it's pleasant
to be home, 25, your Gandhi-cap
shining with recognition, and your dad
has already picked for you a wife,
your Mitsubishi van disgorges your buddies
upon the picnicking lawn, the new
cookout is set up, piles of the best curry,
high time you reverted to eating Indian,
your pet mynah perched on your shoulder,
and there's loads, pardon me, there's
crores of Kingfisher and Heineken,
no revolution happening on the golf courses,
and the radio is a voice from the sky,
it blares godspeed and says you are doing well.

CAN YOU HEAR ME?

Dad, can you hear me, I'm talking to you across the ocean and the plains of Europe and other geographic features, which means that my voice travels in an arc toward you, but by the time it's near the Caucasus very little of it is left, so I can't be sure if you hear me, the only other hope being for some telepathic shimmering, who knows whether this works or not, though it did seem to work when I was younger, very young, and Mom's brother died in Moscow, and then there was that earthquake in Moldova, the first in a string of earthquakes, and you were away translating, but we could hear you even as the floor quaked, bottles crashed, the television rode into the corner, the hens, dogs and cows outside had flapped, howled and mooed for hours before the quake, wasn't that a kind of telepathy too, who knows how this works, yet things and money are shit and knowledge is gold, you told me, and later you said you were tired of work and were going to die soon, and I cried secretly later, how long ago was it, and at the vegetable shop the cashier lady short-changed us and called you a bear, and you said you were bear enough to bite her, and I wasn't even paying much attention, I guess I was fascinated by the concept of minus seven, and Tom had green eyes and was a linguist, too, his bark was almost human, and you told me, the Bolsheviks took a beautiful idea and fucked it up, but you must feel the beauty of the idea, no, I guess that was when I was older, but right now my crimson young pioneer tie still flies unnoticed in the wind, and, as they say in English, don't trouble trouble until trouble troubles you, though basic humanity is triple essential, and when Tom got run over you let me cut school and we wrapped him in his towel and put him in an old suitcase to bury him in a grove by the No. 10 terminal bus stop, and Mom is taking those tranquilizers because of me, I'm being a pedagogical disaster, you are the only adult I can really talk to, but Mom is against English because she feels it alienates me from her, and she is right, and I stupidly ask her, can't you just learn it yourself so you can understand, and she just cries, and these books published in the West, my God, is that a samizdat, you call this poetry, these whinings of the soul, yeah, but you're not like that, though everybody is complicit, and the next day I went and some scum bastard had dug Tom up and left him on the ground, the old suitcase torn up, the towel missing, this was in Moldova in 1978, but traces of a soul can't flee, and Tom is barking still and playing with his mug, Tomik, back to the balcony, says Mom, and I am walking with you, my big Enlightenment figure, I say I believe that things are objective and if a moment happens, it happens for the whole universe simultaneously, and you tell me it is a thought worth writing down.

ART FOR WHOSE SAKE?

Should I go blind if I must preach to moles?
Mute if to mollusks? Should such exercise
as counsel with a few hard-working souls
acquit my psyche in all taxpayer eyes?
Should I be delegitimized by law?
Should I be even brought before the courts
of public conscience, sworn to stand in awe
of its authority, and what is worse,
be asked to take my plea and act elsewhere,
to argue with the devil if I please
or go berserk in either hemisphere,
producing art for my own sake, but tease
with genuine pain and yet without complaint
that landscape of the soul, so hard to paint?

CABBIES, CAFES, CAPEK

Cabbies, cafés. Capek.
Capes' capias. Capos.
Caves, cavies, ceibas,
cèpes... Cepheus chafes
chapbooks, chapeaux, chapes.
Chavez, cheapies, cheapish
Chiapas chibouks, Chippewas
chives, chivies, chivvies,
Chuvash civics, cobias,
coffees, copecks, copes,
copies copious, coupes,
copes, coveys, cowboys,
cowfish, cowpeas, cowpox,
coypu cubbies, cubes,
cubic cubics, cuppas,
Gabes, gabies, gaffes,
gapes, gibbous gibes,
giveaways, gives, gobies,
goboes, gobos, gopik
guavas guffaws guppies,
gyves, japes, javas,
jayvees, Jebus jeebies,
jefes, jewfish jibes,
jiffies, jives, jubas,
kaffiehs, kapoks, kappas,
kavas kebbocks, kebbucks,
keepbacks, kepis, kibbehs.
Kibbes kibbis kibes.
Kibosh kivas Kobuk.
Kopeks, Kopeysk, koppies
Koufax, kybosh Quebec!
Quipoes safes Saivas,
Sapphics saves savvies.
Sawbucks sawfish scabies.
Scabious scapes, sci-fis,
scopes, Scopus scubas.
Seabags, seabass, Seabees,
seappus, sepias, Sepik.
Sepoys shapes shaves!
Shavies. Sheaves. Sheepish
shipways, shivahs, Shivas,
shives shoepacks, shoppes
shoves showbiz, sieves

skewbacks, skives skivvies
skybox, soapbox, Soaves
sofas, Sophies, sowbugs,
squawfish, subfusc, Subic
subways, suffix, Sufic
swabbies swaybacks, sweepbacks,
swipes: xebec xebecs
zebus, Zouaves zwiebacks.

SOLITUDE

There is no disillusionment but this,
that all you are and do, whatever you
are known for or unknown for, liquid basis
for inadequate self-hypothesis, who,
barely responsible for even your thoughts
reflected in these puddles of the streets,
are standing scruffy here in your much rained-on
rectangular flabbergasted coat, who see
the world's obnoxious liver from a taxi,
repeated in this wan medallion, don
the sulks, who knows addictive reasoning
in this café and that, who prowls the piers
without legitimate learned business, cling
to the objective certainty of your tears
that there's no blessed chance in strutting hell
(where you are stuck) that you can even tell
that there's behind you an exactly other,
your prototype, been-before, essential twin,
and yet you're skies apart, like sun and sin,
and thoroughly unseen by one another
where elms suck streetlamps for that shady light
which surely is the very milk of night.

PARROTS

as a parrot
in a bush
to another
parrot said
man things
are not bad
what more
could we wish
and how
they'll come
then go
red feathers so
eat a mango
for now
the key
is to be
perfectly
undetectable
delectable
twee

A VISCERAL YES

Think of all the things a noncom can do to a private.
But that still leaves room for purity.
I took a test of English as a fourteenth language.
Charity begins at home,
that's the subject of my poem!
Wild cows work my engine.
Wild daydreams arise,
surprisingly ablaze with Paris.
You wanna find yourself a moister oyster?
Yes, what's up, priceless!
Nutcracker my ass.
I want to be a wooden peg.
I want to be a wooden peg
in the Woodberry Poetry Room.

ON THE CITY

White chains of snow over the city's limbs
distract the crows. Black slush is full of fire.
Impervious to the wind, a Volga climbs
uphill with taut tenacity of tire,
slowing at icy places. In twilight
a few scattered pedestrians stomp and steam,
rubbing their ears red in a sprinted flight
to the Metro from a capitalist canteen.
The parks begin to yawn, where statues still
stand half-emphatically, as if leaning
toward the vacuum of a lost empire.
Large are the workings of the general will,
but in the early February evening
Moscow's true stars are menacingly clear.

FAMILY VALUES

This is I,
married guy,
and this is
my Mrs.

I love it when we talk,
foreplay, play and done,
but I sometimes alone
chastely go for a walk.

Cute girls sail by,
and well I'm a guy,
yet my attention
to them is none.

When I was single
I liked to mingle,
but in my married life
I save it for my wife.

Love is our action
in our home of homes,
but on a stroll my distraction
is to think me some poems.

See me walking down the street
with a Camel on my lip,
with an eye in every socket,
and a rhyme in every pocket.

EPIPHENOMENONA

A soul's rhymed résumé
shreds to a petaled clause.
Adieux to Mallarmé.
We fold him to a pause.

Objects emerge adrift
out of themselves, boil over.
Life rattles like a lift
in an express land-rover

across a landscape of
shuffled with wakeful landmarks
high Netherlands, tough Denmarks
of pluck and love.

All memories lay thick
dabs of a paintbrush
over a canvas quick
with horse and rosebush

in hue and dew. Their ruby
eyes have no trouble
discerning in my hobby
a whirring crucible.

Insomnia, my friend!
Our ultraviolet
bonds inform the heart
with certain violent

moments. It's time to snooze,
but from the operation
of the imagination
what do we stand to lose?

What do we stand to gain
from always wanting not to
want? Let us rather want.
Even in vain.

VEGAN SYMPHONY #9

Roaring roast cake with bean base spareribs for me,
carottes étouffées medium rare,
I like them a tad undercooked, still red
with sap, tea leaves in olive oil,
strawberry sushi flummoxed
to the point of deliquescence,
or better still, freshly picked
cucumber rolls to match
the lettuce steak, mesquite broiled
to a crunchy andante, with all
organic granola salsa, nuts
nutritious to the max, and then of course the
soypork casserole with legs
of boletus, and tofu chops on a platter
of tomato paste base salmon with
a sprinkling of beet juice droplets,
all served with a rich broccoli broth.

UNCANNING

for Vladimir Sorokin

The grid of the categories, the mani-
fold of the senses. So lovely,
so thoroughly true.
The arch-opaqueness beyond,
wrapped up in itself,
lit through with its own concerns,
invisible from here.
Bye-bye, stay there. Bye,
immanently, permanently,
Immanuel. In yourself,
behind the shell
of your present representation.
And from here,
ah Husserl mein Husserl,
but I assure you consciousness is
a graveyard of words.
Memory cemetery.
words/worms
This can of words
capisce
Wormsworth?
Words are necronyms,
names of that which is dead.
Crass
grass boutique lampade,
obnox. wall decoration -
but from here to there
is nowhere, is unknowable.
'Hind a wall. Knoch Knoch,
who's there?
what's there?
But here, in the consciousness,
wild larvae swell
torquing and swiveling their terms.
We're expert at worminology,
at wormomatopoeia. Thick variously colored
worms. I too have shuddered
as they crawled down my neck,

as they sped their way through my eyes
and fingertips,
as they restructured the upper and lower components
of my being. Worms of love,
delicately sensuous, worms of tears,
worms of envy, of despair,
of pain, of echolalia,
squirms of worms of ejaculation.
Worms of do you believe in extraterrestrials,
of they will stop at nothing.
Worms of nothing.
Worms of the logical nothing.
Worms of resentment.
Worms of everything. Of
have you forgotten our agreement,
of there is something behind the appearance of a candle,
worms of the fine structure of the spider's leg.
Worms in toto, clear, calling
at their slow fast speed,
intermittently aglow,
never stopping their toil.

A WHITE SONNET

The snags of snow in the road's melting plank,
the café lights' unnecessary swank,
the inappropriateness of a photograph
and the superfluousness of an autograph.
A movement must begin, the tricky know-
how of the snow not being a factor now.
To think, to ponder with a heightened brow
at 33 the unity of snow.
To linger in the window. To discuss
an answer to the what I'm doing here
question of questions. The sarcastic flair
of a mind process captured by the snare
of how things are, of how things are with us -
before it is too late to catch the bus.

GABLES, SABLES, STABLES AND JUNE

I've learned my craft from the religious poets.
Enticing me with buns of fire, great lotus-
flung eyes, platinum claws and olivaceous skin,
the Muse seems slightly annoyed at my exuberant
piety, my worship of the thin-perfumed comportment
and imperious charisma of her person. Jade long
initially, shadows scurry away under the table, squirm
(sliced to gauze flakes by her hot illumination,
scattered like tear-stained jasmine petals) and dissolve
while I ventriloquize my mind into dithyrambs,
wonder about her cosmetics, focus on her costume,
then on her disposition, entertain possibilities
and know not what to do with my love-tormented,
insignificant, stiff, love-abiding protuberant self.
Questions hang in the air, like hair. Have you ever
encountered this problem, comrade? Don't tell.

Listen. When she my lips refills with burnings wild,
with shame and yearning replenishes my limbs and all,
and here we omit a whole scene of passionate
love-making and continue with images of ripe
erotic symbolism captured in a variety of forms, either
printed on organdy, or carved in orangewood,
or inlaid with lucent gems and initialed in goldleaf,
generally intended for a vivid yet soothing effect
and clarified visualization. She pours the Beaujolais
and Scotch, we spark up and share a spicy old cigar
and amuse ourselves with good conversation.
She is not really up to date on the subject of movies.
I, on the other hand, happen to be, as it turns out,
all the rage among her eight sisters, all eager
to meet me more closely, giving my sweetie
the trouble of jealousy. Bitches, covetous egoists.
Forgetting them soon, letting them quietly drop
through the oubliette, relaxing, finally relaxed,
our faces marked for comfort by the flames,
we read a while by the fireplace in self-oblivion.

Mysterious as tabloids (they're my fave)
are the possible worlds of which we rave, but have
no direct experience, though are tempted by them,
almost as if trying implicitly to ratify them
with the materials of the imagination. Heck of a task for
a young pen-pusher poet, who has nothing to ask for
but information, if he tried to get sidelights
on those worlds by checking out some tabloid headlines.
Those are, "Atlantis Rises Back." "Cockroach Rapes Cop."
"To Win at Cards Call Now for Your Lucky Tabletop."
"Synthetic Babies Manufactured by Boston Mafia."
"Space Alien Votes for Clinton, Claims Rights of a
US citizen." "Blue Terror Grips Moon." And finally,
"G-spot Wins Fresh Scientific Victory."

That last one wakes me up. I crumple the cacophonic rag
and send it direct into the fireplace, where it goes whoosh
by full consignment. You bring in chilled strawberries
from the kitchen, pink monstrosities that deliquesce.
Pink monstrosities that deliquesce so well. Nothing but
pink monstrosities that are pretty good at deliquescing.
We meditate on them a jiffy. Then we go
and get dressed for a horse ride. I almost decide to ride
sidesaddle, out of my solidarity with the feelings
of my Muse's gender, but she vigorously talks me out of it.

Silver Quiver is a good horse, he carries her with perfect poise.
My Muse looks swift and crisp and beautiful, her crop
only adding to the hallucinatory charm of her authority.
She brought her crop back from Bujumbura, capital
of Burundi, a port at the N end of Lake Tanganika,
where she passed herself off as an international journalist.
My own equine friend, the charger Counterforce, likewise
plies his trade with habit and mastery. Out the castle gate and into
the village and on and on across a wide ribbon of heath and into
a nearby grove which is perched like a shrine within the sunshine.
The hurricane of her tresses rejuvenates my heart, clears it of sin,
obliterating - with a single sweep of light - decades of decadence.
The entirety of experience pours like a cataract into purification.
The branches yield, they yield all the way. They yield.
She drives me mad. It will be a while before we return.

Upon our regaining Abbe Hall, it is sunset. Our friend
the Frenchman is not about to be seen. His companion,
whom we encounter at tea in the garden, informs us
rather calmly, "Monsieur le capitain, he practices the shots."
Mister the captain, good for him. Let him practice.
We shall dine together later. The captain's companion says,
"I expect so." We bid the Frenchman's companion bye
for now and go eagerly into the vivarium, where my Muse
will now feed the sables. This is totally the wrong time to
feed them, but there's no stopping her, because it's such fun.
Incidentally, we have many other pets too, but I don't
want to talk about them here. I'll tell you about them later.
For now let's hear her talk about things.

Tell me, captain, she says at dinner, why are you Frenchmen
so sensitive about the passions? And without waiting for him
to speak, she answers herself, it is because of the chivalric
experience of medieval French history. I recommend,
forgive her, captain. She is just a Muse, my little sweet flower,
my darling baby girl, so youngly naive. If you try to seduce her,
I will kill you, you frog bastard. Come now, relax, relax,
mon vieux, my good man. Look, there is sauerkraut
on your lapel. Nighty-night. Sleep well, we will
see you tomorrow morning on the golf strip. Put away
your rapier. This is Abbe Hall, not Brussels. Take it easy, OK?
Sleep tight. Say hello from us to your companion.

Back in our chamber, which you may call the penthouse,
there is more kissing and hugging and loving and almost fainting
with love and then calming down, until the Muse dozes off
in my arms as I tell her some fairy-tale which I make up
even as I'm telling it, even as I'm telling it to her,
whichever is the correct construction. The tale
is about her and me cast onto the scene as two little Japanese
playing in a narrow street in the old samurai days,
in a past life or something. On a classic miniature
(which seems extremely rare and actually Chinese)
Japanese nature overhangs us with its majestic familiarity,
making us look both timeless and lost in time,
a little Japanese girl and boy playing with a funky balance toy,
whatever that is, in the remote days of the Southern Song Dynasty,
as it turns out according to the inscription. Boy, my Muse here
sure could cock a squeak about it being all Chinese vs. Japanese,
but it's OK, cuz she is asleep by now, and I'm quiet.

Her breath is warm on my cheek. I can hear the sudden
thunderstorm outside and the patter of rain on the open window.
It is magnificently fresh. I try to grasp and remember
that which scintillates at the very margins of the intellect,
similar to a far candlelight, only more complicated,
as I'm being won over by sleep. It's like a clear obscurity.
It's like a chucked problem vs. a chuck it problem.
Is there really a difference? Moreover, do the acacias in Moldova
remember us as we were? Through the night's light rapping,
love, one can almost hear our adventurous dreams take off
up along tall lightning bolts into a now completely different sky.

DITTY OF WISDOM FOR BEN MAZER

> *Where's my blaster?*
> *Where's my blazer?*
> *Where's my redolent Ben Mazer?*

Lavish, hang on lavish,
never say we'll vanish,
never say without a blinking trace.
Keep them tables turning,
old lang candles burning,
shining tough complicity in our face.

For we drive the odd car
and we bibe our vodka,
and we can untwirl what's tightly twirled.
Th' United Roses at our meetings
send out translucent greeings
to th' Federated Lilies of the World.

As we mess with orders,
jump illegal borders,
dream forthcoming volumes on the shelf,
through such pointed messing
life becomes a lesson,
like, a lesson to others in itself.

Night's misleading bushes
shall shoeshine our tushes
with their aromatic loveliness
as we recite our poetry
to a mad boa mag woa tree
in the park's moon-flooded emptiness.

We, no-nonsense buddies,
honest, lean and courteous,
redolent of junipers in bloom,
view the wide horizon
bright with starry eyes on
on the lam with sanitary broom.

Lavish, hang on lavish,
lay on French and Spanish,
Latin, Greek and Russian, and I'll bet
our wabbaggidda wooberrings
and maggaggitta drooberings
no gentleman nor lady will forget.

DEATH OF THE LYRIC

They say the lyric is dead,
the lyric is dying.
Lyric in Deadminster,
as they say.
In Deadsville.
Death,
on the other hand,
is by itself lyric.
Lyricful.
Lyrescent.
So they kind of
replace each other,
death
and the lyric.
The lyric died
into death,
but death will lyrebird
into its own lyric. It's
boysenberry essential
that I speak to you
immediately,
because the lyric
is dead.
Who killed the lyric,
but spared
the panegyric?
The lyric may be dead,
but its death
is alive.

IT NEVER LEAVES

The mind's a rolling plate.
Its formula is plot.
The crow is by the gate.
The tea is plenty hot.

Where are the crow and cow?
They're in a shock of hay.
Myself, I am right now.
Tomorrow's yesterday.

To see is to believe.
To know is to achieve.
The firmament is deep.
The house is fast asleep.

Rosemary leaves are eyes.
No curtain is drawn tight.
The moon is no surprise.
The telephones are night.

Life is a sudden rain
across the lunar eaves.
And nothing is again,
although it never leaves.

STATUS

back drowned well grounded note
from here uncompass and then it travels
mag tragic hallucination buttermilk
infiltrations and then tragic again
but in a different sort of spare
moist tragic
sporting billable ties
mark the big mansion approach
to the arts and then the limos
are in themselves, stretch limos
in themselves, unknowable,
you might say, to pure reason
not only but also taking away
from the character rose caramel
vision of reality
from behind palatial glass
piled high through the sky
in the museum of art monstrosity
winds may reach higher of course
but wind is no competition
to who got plenty of his own
a plethora of his own you might say
wind
no competition to skyscraper
cuz in this city
nobody cares that nobody
understands nobody
let alone having the chip on my shoulder
no one will have a chip off my desire
except to go into their eye and explore
as how I am not at all from here
and my bathysphere drifts askance
into the sly rockage of
the salmon run of my fountain of joy of sorrow
bent out
into an altogether corporeal shape

ANIMAL

I am an animal
with no immortal element of soul
and several barking teeth through which I lie
each fucking day.
This is an extreme point of alienation,
a feeling that cannot be faked.
Motto: crazy but not a crank.
I've got no retirement plan. Fuck retirement!
Just vowels of the pain
and wows (woughs) of the heart.
When the time comes I will
kindly take a moment to die.
Take for example
rivers gnawing away at the bone
of reality, where it (nothing)
hurts and seems real,
yet it hurts nothing that it exists.
For example, you don't know where to go
and the bar is closed
(your vertigo told you to go to a bar),
and you go to a train instead
and ride a few lines down the wintry autumn.

DODGING 1985

The user interface has the following format. Upon accessing the URL, the user sees a welcome message with some explanation of the service provided. The user is prompted to enter his or her name, date of birth, *When everything else fails, try something new.* and email address, *For instance, try the central mental hospital,* then to left click on the *sit back and mumble enjoying the belle vue* submit button. Based on *until the nurse has counted you all.* this information, the CGI script *Our group files in fresh from the courtyard walk,* generates "on the *a pageant of male flesh in ugly dress.* fly" an appropriate horoscope *There's bundles of excitement but little talk.* reading for the end user, *The chess-players are breaking out their chess.* or displays the logs *No one to mention the Afghan War. The state,* and user statistics if *crumbling, buys me my sparse and forkless lunch.* the current user is *This latest novel fails to kill my worries.* the site admin. Parse CGI *The Plexiglas window withstands a teenage a punch.* variables (or *God, I must prove completely nuts, by fate* lookup logged record) to *unfit for active military service.* obtain user's birthday. Parse user's stats, verify and save to log file. Compute user's Zodiac sign based on birth date. Print personalized greeting. Generate a horoscope reading and send it to user's browser} else if (user == administrator) {compute stats.

ALIENATION

As publishers and information vendors are striving to cope with a host of new challenges imposed by the digital age, the costs of maintaining robust multiple production and delivery systems skyrocket. Meanwhile, most *I feel like a spy in my own home city.* Web-generated publishing revenues *I know my drop is somewhere very near,* have been growing quite a bit *boasting fraternal hospitality,* slower than initially expected. In these *with distance growling though a thin veneer.* challenging times, we *It feels as if this ancient friend and I* have learned by practice that *were agents in some ticking action drama* ePublishing thrives and *with heavy accents. One of us must die.* generates healthy returns when *There is no love lost in this cinema.* done correctly. Indeed, we have *But we put up appearances, emplotting,* helped it happen time and *as critics say, and also exemplifying* again. Modernize your creation *some moral content or a public lie.* and publication processes. *Yet obligation draws us closer, blotting* Automate aggregation, review *out petty distinctions, thus verifying* and workflow into a seamless *our mutual, as yet unbroken alibi.* production line. Build a transparent multichannel delivery environment. Capture all existing revenue models and keep adding new ones. Integrate with your back office smoothly, without a headache. Bring a little sangfroid to the technology blizzard.

ANAMNESIS: ANOTHER MEDIUM

The Risk Nexus Station allows you to run various analytics and what-if scenarios on your portfolio as a whole and on any combination of assets within it. These reports and simulations are performed in real time over a live connection to our fully exhaustive repositories of pre-calc risk info. Our Risk Nexus Station's a neat, tightly integrated toolset that combines ease of setup and visualization w/ cutting edge analytical/predictive & reporting capabilities. We developed the Risk Nexus Station to provide asset&$$ managers with affordable access to the power of fast quantitative applications, which until now was the exclusive privilege of large financial corporations & banks. Now you too can evaluate your risks! The Risk Nexus®, the most basic data-driven concept underlying the Risk Nexus Station, gives you for any instrument a nice clean view of its historical market price series.

Dear Dad, I wish that I could write a verse
as if finding occasion to disburse
some universal wisdom, but I can't
find the right words, and I hence I sit and pant,
and think, and then no longer think, and cry,
and let the napkin wipe my eyelids dry.
Full of the fallacies to which I'm prone,
I stare, transcontinental and alone,
into Platonic mirrors, where, sublime,
we float on memories of distant time
all the way back, to where I found a key
in a sunlit street puddle in Sochi. We
both laughed, and what you said I still recall -
the thought that I remembered first of all.

MONKEY TIME

for Diana Eck

There's a Durga temple in Benares they call
Monkey Temple, because of the monkeys who inhabit it
cheek by jowl with the human race.
The monkeys occupy the upper-tier gallery
on top of the thick wall enclosing the temple and engineer
dazzlingly brilliant sorties into the human world. They
wait for prasad to be laid out in front of the ten-handed,
multiweaponed goddess, flower-festooned
slayer of demons, but not of monkeys. Then they wait
for the priest to commence the circling of the lamp
and the ringing of the brass handbell, and then
with what may have long become a Pavlovian reflex
the sly critters descend into the courtyard,
forming themselves into two groups. Members of one
fling themselves acrobatically upon the temple bells,
raising a tremendous racket, inducing
considerable annoyance in the humans. The humans,
except for the Brahmin at work, act as one herd.
They turn and try to shoo the beasts away
with harmless stones, while the other monkey platoon
overruns the sacramental food, makes tracks
with it, sharing with kinsmen bananas and tangerines
back at their architecturally attractive, impregnable
superior station. When provoked, they are capable
of anything, the tricksters. The temple administration
tolerates them for theological reasons, but is powerless
to impose significant constraints, and the diarchy
of hanuman and human stands unshakable.

Today I decided to brave the outer gallery and walk
all the way around, so as to examine the courtyard
from above, armed myself with a thick stick, negotiated
the man-betrayed stairs and stepped
on monkey turf. All hell broke loose as I took
the first few strides into their dominions. There were
monkeys screaming from all sides, baring white
obnoxious fangs amid leaping green indignation. Even the tiny
cubs yammered their guts out and came on

closest to where I had stopped. I unpocket
a breakfast apple and put it down on the floor. How long ago
did man walk here last? Ten years? Fifty years? Is this
where Kipling found the *bandarlog*? One must admit he knew
his stuff, old Rudyard. On a second's reflection I bail out
in self-preservation, my evolutionary brothers ululant in pursuit.
Propelled to safety, I then smile and catch my breath,
shaking the sweat from my brow. I gaze
into the laughing stare of the awesome wife of Shiva,
her benevolence permitting me to pass without harm.
Leaving 2 rupees for the servants of her house, I bow
out. With my right hand I touch the temple step,
then touching my forehead. I put on my shoes.
Continuing all the way down to the river ghats,
I keep on conversing in my head with the monkeys.